DISNEY

BEVERLY HILLS CHIHUAHUA 2

DISNEY
BEVERLY HILLS CHIHUAHUA 2

Adapted by Sarah Nathan

Executive Producers Sara E. White, Mike Callaghan

Produced by Brad Krevoy

Based on characters created by Jeff Bushell

Written by Dannah Phirman & Danielle Schneider

Directed by Alex Zamm

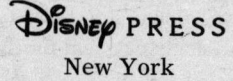

DISNEY PRESS

New York

CHAPTER ONE

Diamonds and sequins glittered in the California sun as the A-list crowd of Beverly Hills gathered for the most talked about wedding of the season. No one was prouder than Vivian Ashe, the hostess of the wedding. While she couldn't really take credit for the couple getting together, she had orchestrated this blissful event, which was being held at her house. Vivian—or Viv, as everyone called her—used her handkerchief to wipe away her tears and caught Sam Cortez's eye. Her landscaper looked dapper in his black tuxedo. Across from him stood Viv's niece, Rachel Ashe. Rachel smiled lovingly at Sam, and Viv wiped her eyes again.

"I can't believe this day is here," Aunt Viv gushed.

"Ladies and gentlemen," the preacher bellowed to the elite crowd. "We are here today to celebrate the union of two very special individuals. Two souls that shall become one, and only shine more brightly together."

The preacher smiled at the crowd and then looked to the bride and groom. "Won't you please join me in bringing together in marriage a much beloved couple," he said. "Chloe and Papi."

The two Chihuahuas gazed into each other's eyes. Chloe looked beautiful in a gorgeous white gown. And Papi fit the part of the dashing groom in a sophisticated black tuxedo.

"Aye, Chihuahua!" Papi exclaimed, looking at his bride-to-be.

"Oh, Papi!" Chloe gasped.

In the front row, three of Chloe and Papi's closest friends stood at full attention. Delta, a tiny poodle, was decked out in her favorite dress. Next to her was Biminy, a Yorkie, in her finest designer outfit. And Sebastian, in a fancy tuxedo and a top hat, was the best-dressed pug at the party.

"I'm just so happy for them," Sebastian said, sniffling.

"Always a bridesmaid, never a bride," Delta grumbled.

"You may all be seated," the preacher told the crowd. The guests did as they were instructed and took their seats. The preacher looked around at the audience and then added, "Sit!" and all the dog guests obediently sat down as well. "Chloe and Papi, do you take each other to love and honor, in good times and in bad, in wet nose and dry nose, as long as you both shall live?" he asked.

Both dogs barked their replies enthusiastically. "I do!"

The preacher grinned. "I now pronounce you husband and wife!"

Papi and Chloe nuzzled lovingly as everyone cheered.

"A toast to the newlyweds," Biminy said as she looked over at Chloe and Papi during the reception. The couple was sitting together next to their wedding cake, gazing into each other's eyes. "They're perfect together. Like Romeo and Juliet," she said with a sigh.

"Or Dolce and Gabbana," Delta chimed in, thinking of her favorite designer duo.

Sam and Rachel passed by the dogs to stand with Aunt Viv. "You really outdid yourself, Aunt Viv," Rachel said. "This is the most spectacular wedding I've ever been to!"

"Oh, Rachel! Isn't it just *perfection*?"

Viv boasted. She turned to Sam, who was standing next to her niece. "I love the arches, and the rosebush topiaries are *flawless*. You are a landscaping genius."

"Thanks, Viv," Sam said, blushing a little. "I wanted to do something special for your Chloe and my Papi on their big day."

"Only the best for my little girl," Viv said, smiling. She blew a kiss across the yard to Chloe. "I want to spoil her rotten before I have to leave her for so long."

A look of sadness flashed across Sam's face. "I can't believe you and Rachel are spending six months in the rain forest," he said. "That's pretty intense."

"Are you kidding?" Viv squealed. "We'll be looking for rare plants that could cure diseases! What could be more fun *and* important?"

Rachel leaned in closer to Sam. "You know I love an adventure," she told him.

A grin spread across Sam's face. "Well, I

promise to take good care of the dogs while you're both gone."

"Speaking of which, tonight is about Chloe and Papi!" Viv exclaimed. "Time to celebrate—let's dance!" She grabbed Sam and Rachel and brought them to the center of the dance floor.

As the three of them sashayed to the music, a waiter placed a large piece of wedding cake on the table in front of Sebastian. "Oh, there goes my diet!" the stylish pug exclaimed as he dug into the supersweet treat. Then the music switched tempo, and the mariachi band began playing a slow, romantic song. Sebastian, Biminy, and Delta all swayed to the music.

A few moments later, Rachel and Sam spun by on the dance floor.

"I never thought my dog would get married before me," Sam said to Rachel as they danced. He swung her around the floor gracefully.

"Maybe it'll be you and me walking down that aisle one day," Rachel said wistfully.

"I'd like that very much, Rachel," Sam said seriously. "Someday . . ." He dipped Rachel and she laughed. They danced through the garden toward the gazebo where Papi and Chloe were also dancing together. Many of Papi and Chloe's dog friends were standing on their hind legs to get a glimpse of the dancing bride and groom.

"You are so light on your paws, *mi amor*," Papi told his new bride.

Chloe blushed. "You're not so bad yourself, my love."

"I call this move the Chihua-*waltz*," Papi bragged, spinning Chloe around. Then he looked deep into her eyes. "Tonight, my heart is bursting," he professed. "I am the happiest dog alive."

"And I'm the luckiest girl ever!" Chloe cried. She glanced around her and then suddenly looked up. "A shooting star!" she exclaimed as the star streaked across the evening sky. "Quick, make a wish!"

Papi shook his head. "What more could I ask for, *mi amor*? I have everything I want."

The newlyweds twirled around to barks and applause from their friends. This was one glorious wedding—and a very happy union. Chloe and Papi shared a smile. It was the best day of their lives!

CHAPTER TWO

A few months after the glamorous wedding, Vivian's yard was back to normal. Well, almost. Chihuahua puppies were frolicking and yapping in the playground.

"Geronimo!" a small, tough-looking pup named Ali shouted as she went down the slide. Another Chihuahua puppy, who was wearing a pink bow on her head, stood at the top of the slide. "Watch and see how it's done, everyone!" she called.

Just then, Chloe walked into the garden

and spotted her puppies playing around in the mud. She watched in horror as Rosa, another one of her puppies, went down the slide and landed in a giant puddle of mud next to Ali.

"Rosa! Ali!" Chloe cried. "What are you kids *doing*?"

"I'm next! I'm next! Me! Me! Me!" Pep, another Chihuahua puppy, shouted. "Look out below!"

"Not you, too, Pep!" Chloe exclaimed.

Just then, Lala, the smallest puppy, zoomed down the slide. "Whoa! This is *scary*!" she cried.

Chloe barked. "Lala, this is crazy! What has gotten into you all?"

Chloe's fifth pup, Papi Jr., was now at the top of the slide and ready to head down. "Look out below!" he announced.

"Don't you dare, Papi Jr.," Chloe warned.

But Papi Jr. ignored his mother and landed in the mud with a splash. He turned his head toward her, trying to look innocent.

Chloe shook her head. "You kids are a mess! I told you I wanted you clean and dressed before we go to the dog park." She looked around the yard. "I don't know where your father is, but when he hears about this, he's going to be so mad," she told the group.

"*Incoming!*" Papi suddenly yelled—from the top of the slide!

The puppies all watched their father go down at full speed. *Splat!* The mud sprayed all over Chloe.

"Oh! Papi!" Chloe complained.

"Oh, my love, I didn't realize you were right there," Papi said apologetically.

Chloe was not pleased. "I like an occasional mud bath, but this is ridiculous," she said.

Papi Jr. moved closer to his mother. "Dad says the ancient Chihuahua warriors would bathe in mud to prepare for battle," he explained to her.

Chloe shot Papi a stern look, then turned to her pups. "You can play warriors later. For now, you kids go get your bath," she ordered.

The puppies began to complain, but Chloe silenced them. "Bath. Now. Or no bacon-wrapped filet mignon for dessert," she told them.

Quickly, the puppies ran toward the house. Chloe glanced down at herself. What a mess! "I better go get washed up . . . *again*." She sighed and trotted off to get ready for the dog park.

"Sorry about the mud, my love!" Papi called. "*Mi amor*, with eyes all aglow, and fur as white as snow—"

"Not anymore!" Chloe called back.

A little while later, Sam came down the grand stairway in Viv's mansion with his car keys in hand. "All right, everyone, who's up for the dog park?" he called out.

"We are!" the puppies barked excitedly.

Rosa, Lala, Pep, and Ali came out to greet Sam. Each one was showing off her fashionable outfit with pride.

Papi looked at his daughters lovingly. "Girls, you are all gorgeous like your mother," he said proudly.

"Thanks, Daddy," the girls replied.

Chloe took a quick look around. "Where's Papi Jr.?" she asked worriedly. "Papi Jr.?" she called.

From behind a vase, a small yelp sounded. "I'm not coming out," Papi Jr. said.

Papi trotted over to the vase. "Come on, buddy! Let's see your outfit."

"This is so embarrassing. I look ridiculous," Papi Jr. grumbled. He slowly came out from behind the vase, sulking.

Papi gasped as he took in the blue-and-white sailor outfit complete with hat, large collar, and little booties. Papi turned to

Chloe. "No way! No son of mine wears clothes like that!"

Relieved that he wouldn't have to go out in public with the hat, Papi Jr. yipped happily. "Thanks, Dad!"

"All right, let's move out. Last one to Sam's car is a bag of kitty litter!" Papi yelled. The puppies excitedly ran out the front door. No one wanted to be *kitty litter*!

A few minutes later, Sam and the dogs arrived at the park. Chloe immediately noticed all the diamond-encrusted collars and silk leashes that the other dogs seemed to have. And some of them even had butlers who dutifully placed toys and set out picnics for their doggie masters!

Chloe continued to take in the scene. A woman walked by pushing her dog in a baby stroller and carrying a parasol to keep the sun out of her pet's eyes. A collie at the far end of the park was pressing an automatic tennis-ball launcher, and his doting maid was fetching the balls! And a butler was presenting a bone to a large husky, to see if it was to the dog's liking!

Sam let the puppies off their leashes. "You kids go play," he told them.

"That's right. This place is very exclusive," Chloe said to her pups. She surveyed the park and spotted her friends Sebastian, Delta, and Biminy. Chloe ran over to greet them.

Sebastian was in the middle of a story. "So I said, 'Honey, I only chase important cars,'" he was telling his friends. Just then, a butler came over. "Lunch is served," he announced, presenting a platter of sushi to them.

"Hi, everyone," Chloe said.

"Chloe!" Sebastian squealed. "You have to join us. This *hamachi* is *faboo*!"

Chloe looked at the spread before her friends. "Looks delish," she commented.

Delta pointed across the park. "My, my," she said. "It looks like your better half is relandscaping the park."

Chloe looked over to where Delta was pointing. Papi was excitedly digging into the ground. "That's my Papi," Chloe said, smiling. "He always leaves a lasting impression."

Across the park, Papi stopped digging for a moment and looked up at his pups. "Do you know what I was just doing, kids?" he asked.

"Digging!" the puppies cried excitedly.

"That's right," Papi said, nodding. "One day, you will all be landscaping dogs like me, but before that, you will have to master the fine art of digging."

Rosa jumped up and down excitedly. "I can dig, Papa. I'm good at everything," she boasted.

"*Bueno*," Papi told her. "Now dig, my puppies! Dig with passion, dig with love, dig as if your life depends on it!" he cried.

As the puppies dug, grass and dirt sprayed everywhere. Unfortunately, some of that dirt flew onto a perfectly coiffed white poodle named Appoline. "You *eee-diots*!" she screamed in a French accent.

Papi and the puppies turned to see who was yelling at them.

"You got me dirty!" Appoline shouted furiously.

Papi rushed over to the tall poodle. "Pardon me, senorita," he said sweetly. "My children got a little carried away with their digging."

"Who *zaid* you could speak to me?" the snobby poodle barked.

Over at the picnic blanket, Chloe sensed trouble. Her ears perked up, and she spotted Appoline yelling at Papi. Her three friends watched as Chloe raced over to her family.

"You look like a stray! How did you even get in here?!" Appoline told Papi.

Just then, Chloe approached. "Papi, what's going on?" she asked.

"*Quel terrible!*" Appoline cried. She gave Chloe a disgusted look. "As if there weren't *enough* of you peasants. Your little fluff balls are running amok."

"Hey!" Papi Jr. cut in. "Who are you calling fluff balls?"

"You tell her, son," Chloe said proudly.

"Shoo!" a well-dressed woman named Colleen Mansfield cried as she ran over to Appoline. She was *not* happy. "Leave my dog alone!" she demanded.

The sudden commotion got Sam's attention and he walked over, concerned.

"What's the problem here?" Sam asked, approaching Colleen.

Colleen gave Sam a long look up and down. "You know, this park is for Beverly Hills residents only. Don't you have dog parks where you live?" she snipped.

"Hey, we have a right to be here," Sam said defensively.

"Oh, really?" Colleen said in a snooty tone. "Well please keep your . . . *animals* away from *Mademoiselle Marie Appoline Bouvier*. She's a prizewinning show dog." Colleen cooed to Appoline as if she were a baby. "*And* a three-time champion of the Beverly Hills Dog Show." Colleen thought back to that glorious moment when her dog had been in the spotlight for winning the prized title. Then she glanced over at Sam. "She can't handle stress."

"Then how does she handle you?" Sam muttered.

Colleen turned on her designer-shoe heel. "Come, Appoline! We're done here!" she announced, storming away.

Sam shook his head in disbelief.

"And *stay* out!" Papi howled as Appoline walked away.

"Yeah!" the puppies all cheered. Chloe gave Papi a playful shove. She couldn't help but smile. She saw her dirt-covered pups looking up at her. When it came to prizes, she felt as if she had won first place for best family—and certainly for the *dirtiest* family in the park!

Later that evening, the puppies were once again clean. And now it was bedtime. Gently using his teeth, Papi pulled the blanket over the doggie bed. "Well, my little *banditos*, you've had a very full day. *Buenas noches*," he said, wishing his pups a good night.

But as Papi went to leave the room, the puppies started yapping. "Can't we stay up ten more minutes, Papa?" Ali begged. "Please, please, please!" the other puppies cried.

"Settle down, now," Papi said calmly. "I promised your mama I would put you to bed. She is the love of my life and I would do anything to make her happy."

"Gross! No more love talk," Papi Jr. complained.

"Your mother is everything to me . . . I remember the first time we rubbed noses." Papi sighed, losing himself in the memory.

"*Ewww!*" the puppies cried in unison.

Papi looked at his puppies fondly. "Let me

tell you a story about our great ancestors. They may have had little bodies, but they were known for their huge hearts." He cuddled next to his pups and began to tell the story of the ancient Chihuahuas. "Long ago, in ancient times, inside the huge temples, there were hidden tunnels built just for Chihuahuas to carry messages for their humans. The Chihuahuas were trusted to carry the most precious secrets of their kingdoms. Sometimes they were messages of love," Papi reported.

The puppies envisioned a Chihuahua warrior giving a princess a scroll. They gave their father an eager look, anxious to hear more of the story.

"The Chihuahuas faced great danger to deliver these messages," Papi continued, "but they knew: love is worth *any* risk." Papi looked at his puppies. "Now, my little Chihuahua warriors, love fearlessly and help others share their hearts as well! Good night."

As Papi walked out of the room, he gave a last loving glance at his children. Then he went to look for Chloe. He found her in a luxurious bubble bath with her ears neatly tucked into a shower cap.

"My sweet, you can soak as long as you want. The children are asleep like angels," he said proudly.

"Sounds wonderful," Chloe said, smiling.

"Oh, yes," Papi said, smiling. "Just go ahead and relax all night . . . I have done the deed," he told her.

Chloe narrowed her eyes. "You want me to look at them sleeping, don't you?" she asked knowingly.

"Yes, very much," Papi told her.

Chloe hopped out of the tub and together, the couple went to check on their puppies. But things were not as Papi had expected. There were feathers flying everywhere! All the puppies were wide-awake and digging in their bed!

"*What* is going on in here?" Chloe cried out.

"We're digging tunnels to carry our messages of love," Ali explained.

"Yep, we sure are!" Pep piped up. Rosa stuck her nose through a hole she had dug in the middle of a giant painting that had been hanging on the wall. "It's so romantic," she said.

Chloe looked at her husband, confused. "Papi, what did you say to them?" she asked.

"Oh, just a little something about Chihuahua warriors braving great danger for love," Papi mumbled sheepishly.

Chloe trotted around the disheveled bed. "I sent you in here to calm them down, Papi, and they're more riled up than ever. You have to put your paw down with them sometimes."

"But I don't want to ruin their fun," Papi told her. "Besides, they're just puppies. They don't know any better."

"So it's up to us to teach them," Chloe pointed out. "You can't be afraid to discipline them."

"Afraid? I'm not afraid!" Papi shouted, standing tall. "I just don't like that part. . . ." He trailed off.

Chloe turned her attention to the puppies. "Okay, I want everyone in bed this minute!" she ordered.

All the puppies scrambled back into the doggie bed . . . except Papi Jr. Chloe stared at him. "Don't make me put you back in the sailor outfit, Papi Jr.!" she warned.

He leaped into the bed.

"Sorry, Mama," the puppies said in unison.

Chloe tugged on the blanket with her teeth and covered the puppies. She sighed and then smiled. Being a mom was hard work, but she loved every minute of it!

CHAPTER THREE

As the early morning sun rose in the sky, the puppies scampered down the hallway to the guest bedroom at Viv's house. They pushed open the door and jumped up on the bed to wake Sam. Groggily, Sam opened one eye as he felt Papi Jr. licking his face. Then all the dogs were barking and licking him.

"Okay, I'm up! I know you guys are excited to meet the rest of the family, but at least let me get out of my pajamas," Sam said, laughing happily.

Soon enough, Chloe, Papi, and their puppies were all in Sam's truck heading away from Beverly Hills. As Sam drove out of the neighborhood, the streets started to look different. Houses were closer together and painted in bright colors, and people sat out on their porches with music playing.

Sam turned to see the puppies sticking their heads out of an open window. "What do you guys think of where your dad and I grew up?" he asked.

"I can't wait for you to meet my brother," Papi said to his family.

Papi was very excited to be back in his old neighborhood. He pointed out where he had once hidden a bone, where he had dug his first hole, and where his favorite fire hydrant was. There were so many memories!

Sam parked his truck in front of a brightly painted house, and his mother came running down the front-porch steps.

"Come inside, I have food," Mrs. Cortez said warmly.

"That's why I come home, Mom. I miss your tamales," Sam said with a smile. He walked up with Rosa, Pep, and Lala in his arms and Ali and Papi Jr. following behind. He gave his mother a kiss on the cheek.

"*Que linda!* So cute!" Mrs. Cortez gushed, looking at the puppies. She bent down and picked up Ali and Papi Jr. "Look at these delicious little *taquitos!*" she exclaimed.

"Be careful," Papi Jr. whispered to Ali. "I think she's hungry!"

Sam, his mother, and the dogs made their way inside the house. Mr. Cortez was sitting in a chair in the living room.

"So *these* are the newest members of the family!" Sam's father exclaimed when he saw the puppies. "Pedro! Come here, boy! Come meet your nieces and nephews!"

Papi's brother, Pedro, a sweet and sensitive Staffordshire terrier mix, lumbered into the living room. The dogs greeted him excitedly. But suddenly, Pedro bared his teeth. He looked really angry!

"Ahhhhhh!" the puppies all shouted, hiding behind their parents.

"He's going to eat us!" Lala cried.

The puppies scattered and dove under the furniture. Poor Pedro looked around, confused by the puppies' reaction. He hadn't meant to scare them!

"Dude," Papi said, coming up beside him, "you've really got to work on that smile."

Pedro stopped baring his teeth. He instantly looked like a sweet dog again.

"*That* was a smile?" Rosa asked.

"Chloe, kids, I'd like you to meet *mi hermano,* Pedro," said Papi. Now that Pedro looked friendly, Papi could formally introduce him to his family. He and Pedro high-fived with their paws.

"Hi, everyone!" Pedro exclaimed, trying not to smile and show his scary-looking teeth.

Chloe stepped forward. "Pedro! It's so good to meet you," she said.

"Chloe," Pedro said, admiring her. "You are even lovelier than I imagined. I'm sorry I was not here to greet you. I saw a butterfly in the yard whose wing was caught in a blade of grass, and I had to blow on it to set it free."

The puppies peeked from where they were still hiding. Pedro seemed very sweet!

"How can you and Dad be brothers?" Papi Jr. asked, incredulously. "You don't look anything alike."

Rosa nudged her brother. "They're not *real* brothers, silly," she told him.

"They grew up on the streets together," Ali said, remembering the stories her dad had told her.

"That doesn't make our brotherhood any less real, kids," Pedro told them. "Family is about who you love, not just who you're born to."

"Well said, *mi hermano*," Papi added. "Ah, I love a family reunion."

As the dogs continued to greet each other, Sam surveyed his parents' living room. He saw a stack of mail on the table and quickly thumbed through the bills.

"Dad, what's this?" he asked.

Mr. Cortez turned to his wife and gave her a worried look.

Mrs. Cortez sighed. "We should tell him, Fernando," she said to her husband.

"Tell me what?" Sam inquired.

"Sit down, son. We have to discuss something with you," Mr. Cortez told Sam.

Chloe watched the Cortez family. She led her puppies toward the door. "You kids go in the backyard and play," she said. "It's time for the adults to talk."

Though they groaned and complained, the puppies scampered outdoors, giving the adults some privacy. Chloe and Papi sat at Sam's feet, attentive to every word spoken.

"Oh, Sam, it was awful," Mrs. Cortez said, shaking her head. "These men from the bank—they came in here and said they're taking the house!"

"But how is that possible?" Sam asked, shocked.

"I haven't been able to make the mortgage payments," Mr. Cortez confessed.

"Dad, why didn't you tell me?" Sam ran his hand through his hair. He had no idea that his parents were struggling financially.

"I thought I could catch up with the payments," his father told him.

Outside, the puppies were curious about what was happening inside.

"What are they saying, Papi Jr.?" Rosa asked. Papi Jr. jumped up, but he couldn't reach the window.

"Ugh, I can't see," said Papi Jr. "Wait, I've got an idea!" By standing on his sisters' backs, he was just barely able to see over the windowsill.

Sam paced around the living room. He couldn't believe what he was hearing. "What about the money from all the landscaping jobs?" he asked his father.

Mr. Cortez lowered his head. "Since my back went out, I haven't been able to work," he said. "We've lost a lot of jobs with the company down to just you," he told his son.

"There's got to be somebody we can ask to borrow the money from," Sam said, thinking aloud. "What about Viv?" he asked.

"No, no, no," his father said adamantly. "We will not burden anyone with our problems. This is a family affair."

"Hold still!" Papi Jr. demanded outside the window.

Rosa, who was part of the tower of Chihuahuas, started laughing. "Pep, your paw smells like peanut butter!" she exclaimed.

Pep giggled. "Your nose is tickling my paw, Rosa!"

Papi Jr. looked down. "Shhhh! I'm trying

to listen!" He watched Sam pace around the living room.

"Uh-oh . . . I can't hold you guys much longer!" Ali warned them.

"Oh, no! Oh, no!" Pep shouted, starting to wobble.

"We're going down!" Papi Jr. cried. He went flying as the tower toppled to the ground.

Inside, Mr. Cortez saw fear in his son's eyes. "Don't worry, the Cortezes have always pulled themselves up," he said, trying to reassure his son.

"And if we can't?" Sam asked.

"The bank will take the house," Mr. Cortez replied solemnly.

Pedro hid his head with his paws.

Mr. Cortez continued. "Your mother and I will have to go live with my sister and her family in Arizona," he said.

"But that's so far from here!" Sam cried. "I'll never see you. And they live in that tiny apartment. What will happen to Pedro?" Pedro put his head in Sam's lap just then.

"I spoke to your cousin in Texas. He can go live with them on the farm. He'll have space to run around," Mr. Cortez told Sam.

Papi barked. "They can't split us up!" he cried.

"It's okay, Papi. We'll figure something out," Pedro assured him.

"It's only until we can save up some money," Mr. Cortez added.

All this talk was too much for Mrs. Cortez. "Oh, my heart is breaking," she said. She stood up from her chair and ran out the back door.

Sam's mind was racing. "There's got to be something I can do. We'll go to the bank first thing tomorrow," he declared.

"Good," Mr. Cortez replied. He didn't sound so confident, but he had complete faith in his son.

In the backyard, the dogs were silent.

"They can't lose this place," Chloe whispered to Papi.

Papi's eyes welled with tears. "This was my first home," he said. "This is where I discovered what family was."

"And what it was like to be loved and taken care of," Pedro added.

"Oh, Papi, Pedro, I'm so sorry," Chloe said. She felt awful for them.

"Before this house, we were on the streets." Papi closed his eyes, and in an instant he was back in the alleys with Pedro, looking in garbage cans for scraps of food. Shop owners would shoo them away, and meals were hard to find.

"We had nothing," Papi told Chloe. "Then one day, Sam and his parents adopted us. Suddenly, we had a family."

"I don't even want to think of what your life would have been like without them and this home," Chloe said sadly.

Papi nodded. "That is why we cannot give up without a fight," he said.

"Yeah!" Pedro agreed. "They gave us a home, let's help them keep it!"

"Tomorrow we start the battle to save the house!" Papi declared.

CHAPTER FOUR

After a long day, the puppies were finding it hard to settle down for the night at the Cortez house.

"Okay, everyone to bed," Papi said.

Rosa came up to her father, her eyes wide. "Are you scared about losing this house, Daddy?" she asked.

Papi couldn't deny his sad feelings. "Well, yes, I am," he replied.

"But you're not supposed to get scared," Lala said, coming up next to him.

"You're the dad," Ali reminded him.

"Right . . . Um . . ." Papi stammered nervously. "Well . . . you know who was always brave?"

Papi Jr. charged forward with the answer. "Chihuahua warriors!" he shouted.

"Yes! Would you like to hear a story?" Papi asked.

"Yeah!" the puppies all cheered.

"Once, there was a little baby in grave danger . . ." Papi began. He told them the story of a snake who was about to attack the baby. He looked around at his children, who were hanging on his every word. "Luckily, a brave member of the tribe acted fast," Papi continued. He told them that when the snake was about to strike, the Chihuahua grabbed it and tossed it to the ground. Then Papi paused and looked at the puppies. "And he was a hero to all!" he concluded.

The puppies leaped up to celebrate the heroic story—except Lala, who shuddered.

"I hate snakes," she said, frightened.

Papi Jr. stood tall. "But the Chihuahua wasn't afraid of the snake at all!" he declared. He turned to his father. "Right, Dad?" he asked.

"That's right," Papi said. "So, we should all be like a Chihuahua warrior and have no fear. *Buenas noches, mi perritos*," he said, wishing the puppies good night.

As soon as Papi was gone, Papi Jr.'s head popped up. He turned to the window and sat up straight. There was a vine outside that looked just like a snake. Warrior time!

Downstairs, Chloe sat in front of a roaring fireplace, enjoying some peace and quiet. Papi walked in.

"Go ahead, check. I assure you, they are peacefully asleep," he said, full of confidence.

At that moment, a bark from upstairs broke the silence.

Papi and Chloe tore up the steps to see

what the commotion was about. As the door to the room opened, Papi and Chloe saw utter chaos—wild puppies jumping around and cheering Papi Jr. on!

"Let me guess," Chloe said to Papi. "You told them another story?"

"Look, Mom! Papi Jr. is a brave Chihuahua warrior! See?" Ali explained. She lifted her nose and motioned toward the open window. There was Papi Jr., balancing unsteadily on the edge of a flower box.

"Don't worry, *mi hermanas*, I'll save you from the evil snake!" Papi Jr. cried.

Rosa giggled. "I told him it's just a vine."

Chloe raced to the window. "Come back here this instant!"

Suddenly, the flower box began to buckle under Papi Jr.'s weight.

"Help!" Papi Jr. screamed.

Chloe jumped up. "Papi, do something!" she cried.

One end of the flower box came unhinged

from the window, and then the whole thing snapped. The box plummeted toward the ground—with Papi Jr.! Terrified, Papi and Chloe ran to the window. They could barely make out the figure jumping into the air to catch Papi Jr.! The flower box smashed to pieces on the ground.

Papi and Chloe charged down the steps and raced out the doggy door in the kitchen. When they got outside, the shadowy figure placed Papi Jr. gently down on the ground.

Chloe couldn't believe her eyes—*or* her son's good luck! "Delgado!" she cried. She had not seen her good friend in a long time. She had met the German shepherd in Mexico, and he had been a true friend when she was lost and alone there. Seeing him now and knowing that he had just saved her son was overwhelming.

"I was just in the neighborhood," Delgado said humbly.

"I've never been so happy to see a dog in my life!" Chloe gushed.

"Thank goodness you were here," Papi said with relief. "I am forever in your debt, Delgado."

Chloe turned to her young pup. "Now Papi Jr., you go back to bed this instant. And never do that again!"

Papi Jr. stuck his tail between his legs and scurried inside the house. Before he reached the door, he turned back to his parents. "Sorry, Mama, I was just trying to be a brave Chihuahua warrior, like in Dad's stories," he said sheepishly.

From the room above, Papi Jr.'s sisters were watching the scene below and giggling. Chloe looked up at them and then at their father.

"I guess he didn't read the fine print where I said 'don't try this at home,'" Papi responded.

Just then, Sam and Mr. Cortez rushed

outside in their pajamas. Pedro was by their side, barking loudly.

Sam glanced around the yard and saw the other dogs. "What's going on out here? Is everyone okay?" Sam asked, concerned. Suddenly, his face softened. "Delgado, is that you?" he asked.

Delgado barked.

"I don't believe it!" Sam exclaimed. He hugged his old friend.

"Don't get all mushy on me now," Delgado told him.

Sam stood up and looked at Delgado, amazed. "How did you get all the way here from Mexico?" he asked. "I better call your partner, Detective Ramirez, and find out what's up." He headed back inside with his father to make the call.

"Delgado, how did you find us?" Chloe asked.

Delgado grinned. "I'm a police dog. Tracking is what I do!"

Papi turned to his brother. "Pedro, this is the *amigo* I told you about," he said proudly. "The one who kept *mi amor* safe when she was lost in Mexico."

Stepping forward, Pedro bowed his head. "It's a true honor to meet you," he said.

Before his brother flashed Delgado his famous smile, Papi warned him, "Uh, maybe don't smile, bro."

Chloe moved closer to her good friend. "What are you doing in Los Angeles, Delgado?"

"I'm here on assignment," Delgado reported. "Um, police business, you know . . ." he began.

Chloe's mind was racing. "Oohh, what is it?" she asked excitedly. "Some kind of undercover operation? You're tracking a criminal!"

"It's classified. I can't tell you," Delgado said. "But I *could* use your help. Will you come with me on a special assignment tomorrow?"

"I'd do anything for you, Delgado," Chloe said sincerely. "I know!" she shouted suddenly. "It's a jewel heist, isn't it? Just give me a hint," she begged.

Delgado shook his head and laughed. "I can see you haven't changed a bit, kid."

Inside the house, Sam was getting off the phone with Detective Ramirez.

"So, you met this dog in Mexico and now he found you in *Los Angeles*? Are you wearing meat cologne, or something?" Mr. Cortez asked his son.

"I don't know why he came here," Sam told his father. "But Detective Ramirez said they're wrapping up a big case down there, and they can't pick him up for a few days. I said we'd look after him until they come." Walking over to the back door, Sam whistled for the dogs. In an instant, they all came running. "Come on guys, back to bed."

Papi looked over at Delgado. "We're glad

you're here, my friend. Let's get some sleep. It's been a long day."

Papi watched Delgado and Chloe walk off. He sighed heavily.

"You okay, bro?" Pedro asked, noticing Papi's expression.

Papi hung his head. "I think I messed up tonight, Pedro," he said. "Papi Jr. could have gotten very hurt. I just hope I can be the father that Chloe wants me to be."

"Just follow your heart," Pedro advised. "It will show you the way."

Papi nodded. He hoped Pedro was right. Then he went upstairs to join his family.

The next morning, Sam and his dad arrived at the bank to talk to the manager. Papi came along, too.

"Gentlemen," Mr. Kroop, the manager, began, "I'd like to help you out, but my hands are tied. You are too far behind on payments."

"What are we going to do?" Sam asked, shaking his head.

Papi leaped into Sam's lap. "Why don't you try begging, Sam," he suggested. "It works when I want your burrito."

Mr. Kroop pushed his chair away from the barking Chihuahua. "I didn't realize you brought your dog. Fun. I'm more of a cat person myself." He reached over and held up a framed photograph of a cat. He looked at the picture of the feline lovingly. "Isn't he a cutie?"

Papi glanced over at the photograph of the man hugging a bored-looking tabby cat. "*Now* I know what's wrong with you!" Papi shouted.

"Look, sir," Mr. Cortez said. "This is our home. Our life is there, our memories . . ." He trailed off sadly.

"Our squeaky toys," Papi added.

Mr. Kroop shook his head. "Well, unfortunately, memories don't pay the bills," he replied. "Now, you've received your final notice. Once that happens, the bank can only give you until the end of the month." He leaned forward to look at the calendar on his desk. "That gives you three weeks to get us forty thousand dollars." He looked up at Mr. Cortez and his son. "If you don't get the money by then, the house is ours."

"Forty thousand dollars? No problem," Papi said, feigning confidence. Then he turned to Sam. "I'll start digging in the couch for change."

"We can't come up with all that money in three weeks!" Sam exclaimed.

"Well, I'm sorry I couldn't be of more help, gentlemen, but I have another client waiting. Please, take a free pen for your troubles." He handed them each a pen and then gave Papi a quick pat on the head.

"You better have nine lives if you want to mess with me!" Papi yelled as they walked away from Mr. Kroop.

"A *pen*? They take your house and give you a pen," Sam said, stunned. Papi looked at Sam and Mr. Cortez. Something had to be done!

Meanwhile, Chloe and Delgado had set off for a walk. When Chloe realized where Delgado had taken her, she stopped short. "What are we doing at the police station? What's so secret? Am I some sort of look-out?" she asked curiously.

Delgado didn't answer.

"Oohh, maybe we should have a code word," Chloe suggested eagerly. It had been so long since she'd been on a great adventure! "How about 'jelly bean'? Do we need disguises?"

Delgado turned to his friend. "Chloe, I just need you to *be* here, okay? Because . . ." He took a deep breath. "This is a bad idea. Maybe we should go."

Just then, two German shepherds looked

up from an obstacle course. They surveyed Delgado from the other side of a fence.

"Those two dogs are coming this way," Chloe told Delgado. "Do you know them?"

"What are *you* doing here?" one of the dogs, named Antonio, growled through the fence.

"That's no way to greet someone!" Chloe reprimanded them. "In my circles, a lick on each cheek does the trick."

Delgado looked the two police dogs in the eye. "I just wanted to see you, make sure you were doing okay," he said.

"Is there something you want?" Antonio asked. "Because we really don't have time to talk."

Delgado raised an eyebrow. "Working on a big case?" he asked.

"There's been a string of bank robberies in the area, and we're trying to catch a scent," Alberto, the other dog, answered. "We should go," he told Antonio.

"Maybe I could see you another time?" Delgado asked hopefully.

"You left us!" Antonio cried angrily. "You didn't care about us, so why would we suddenly care about you?"

Just then, an officer whistled. The two dogs took one last look at Delgado and then ran off to their training group.

Chloe was confused. "Delgado, who were those dogs? They were so angry."

"Those are my sons," Delgado said quietly.

"*Sons*?" Chloe asked, stunned. "I didn't know you had sons! Why didn't you tell me this earlier?"

Delgado walked away sadly. Chloe ran to catch up with him.

"I'm sorry I dragged you into this," he said. He shook his head.

"So, there's no secret police mission you need my help with, is there?" Chloe asked him.

"I thought with you by my side, I'd have

the strength to face my boys and tell them the truth," he told her.

"The truth about what?" Chloe asked, even more confused.

"Forget it. I can't change the past now," Delgado said and walked away.

Chloe stared after her friend in shock. *Now* she understood why Delgado had come all the way to California. And Delgado was like family to her. She vowed that she'd be there for him—no matter what.

In the rain forest, Rachel was thinking about Sam when her phone rang suddenly. It was him! She was so relieved to hear his voice. She missed him so much! But as she listened to what Sam's family was going through, she felt awful.

"There's just no way we can come up with the money in three weeks," Sam told her over the phone.

"There must be something we can do,

Sam," Rachel said as she walked through the compound where she and her aunt were staying. "I'm going to ask Aunt Viv."

"No!" Sam said adamantly. "My father is very proud. Borrowing money is something that he just can't do."

"I feel so helpless. I should come home," Rachel told him. She looked over at Aunt Viv, who was carefully examining a rainforest plant.

"This is the one!" Viv cried gleefully.

"Listen, you have to stay there. You and Aunt Viv are doing important work," Sam said.

Rachel nodded. But in her heart, she wanted to be with Sam. "I love you, Sam," she told him. "I'm here for you if you need me. Forever if you wanted," she added.

Sam sat down in a chair in his parents' backyard. He put his hand on Papi's head. "Thank you. You know, I should go," he said to Rachel. "I make for lousy conversation right now. I'll call you soon."

"Okay," Rachel replied sadly. "Good-bye, Sam."

As Sam hung up the phone, his mother came outside, carrying a sweater for him.

A smile spread across Mrs. Cortez's face. "Was that Rachel on the phone?" she asked. "When can I start planning a wedding?" She winked at her son. "I already have a dress picked out."

"Ma," Sam said. "I love Rachel, and I don't want to lose her." Sam slumped lower into the chair. "But I'm worried if we get married I won't be able to give her the life she deserves," he said sadly.

"Sam, all that matters is that you love each other. The rest will work itself out," Mrs. Cortez said sincerely. She smiled at her son and headed back inside the house. Deep down, she knew everything would turn out the way it was supposed to.

Sam reached down to pet Papi. "Oh, man,

Papi," he said. "What do I do? I'm just scared I won't be enough."

"I feel you, man. I feel you," Papi replied, hoping Sam could understand. He put his head in Sam's lap and together they sat, wondering if they could be enough for their true loves.

CHAPTER FIVE

After a lazy breakfast the next morning, the dogs lounged on the couches in the living room. A loud knock on the front door made them all jump to attention.

"Coming! Just a minute!" Sam, still in his pajamas, called as he ran down the stairs to the front door. As he looked through the peephole, he sighed heavily and opened the door.

"Morning!" a very chipper Mr. Kroop bellowed at the front door. "Oops, looks like

I woke you. Sorry," he said. When he saw the disbelief on Sam's face, he thought perhaps Sam didn't recognize him. "I'm Mr. Kroop from the bank," he reminded Sam. "We met the other day."

"How could I forget?" Sam said. "You gave me a pen," he added sarcastically.

Smiling, Mr. Kroop nodded. "And here's a notice for you, too. I'm here to inspect the house since the bank will be selling it once you're out."

Mr. Kroop walked into the house and was met by all the dogs staring at him. He took a step back. "Oh, more dogs . . . lovely," he mumbled. He looked over his shoulder at the inspectors behind him. "Let's get started, everyone!" he directed.

A couple of house inspectors came in and pushed past Sam. They held clipboards and measuring tapes. Just then, Mr. and Mrs. Cortez rushed into the room, wondering what all the noise was about.

"Samuel, what's going on?" Mrs. Cortez asked worriedly.

"They can't just come in here like this!" Mr. Cortez declared as he realized what was happening.

Sam read the notice in his hand. "There's nothing we can do," he said quietly. "They have the right."

Papi wasn't about to let Mr. Kroop and the inspectors upset his family. "Come on, everyone!" Papi called. "They aren't taking this house without a fight!"

The dogs all gathered around Papi. They talked among themselves, agreed to a plan, and quickly spread out around the house.

Papi Jr. took hold of one of the measuring tapes and played a little game of tug-of-war with it.

"Let go! Bad dog!" an inspector yelled. "Very bad dog!"

But Papi Jr. was holding on tight. Ali cheered her brother on. "*You* let go! Bad

Newlyweds Chloe and Papi had a wonderful time
at their wedding!

"You look like a stray! How did you even get in here?"
Appoline asked Papi when he arrived at the dog park.

The puppies settled in for one of their dad's famous
bedtime stories.

When Papi and Chloe learned that their owners were in trouble, they knew they had to do something to help.

Chloe realized that if they won the dog show, they could help their owners.

Pedro strutted his stuff at the dog show.

"I've got all my paws crossed," Biminy told Delta and Sebastian. The stylish Yorkie wanted her friends to win!

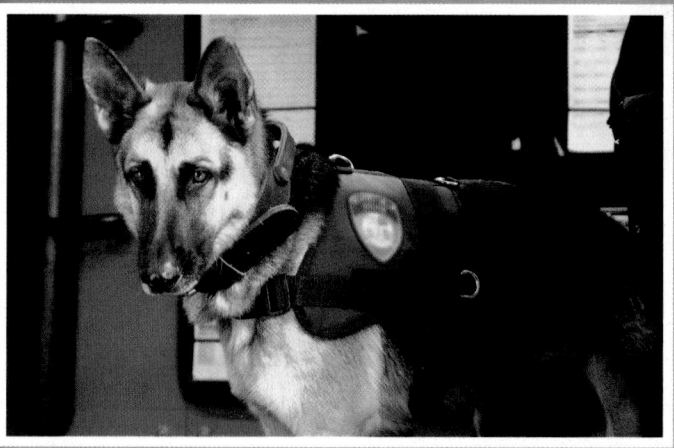

One of Delgado's sons found out there had been a bank robbery in town!

Chloe explained to the dogs in the K-9 unit that her puppies were missing!

Pedro tried to follow the scent of the bank robbers.

Chloe and Papi's puppies sensed there was trouble.

The puppies worked together to try to catch the thieves!

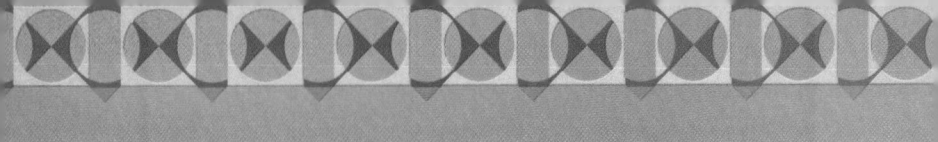

Back home—safe and sound!

lady!" she barked. "Very bad lady!"

"Give me back my tape!" the woman screamed at Papi Jr. She tried to wrestle it away from him.

Just then, Papi Jr. let go of the tape. It snapped back and hit the woman in the face!

"Be careful what you wish for," Papi Jr. said with a smirk.

Meanwhile, Delgado stood by the window in one of the upstairs bedrooms. Outside, an inspector was climbing up a ladder to the window. Delgado barked as loud as he could, and Pedro jumped to his side.

Pedro flashed the inspector one of his trademark smiles.

The instant the inspector saw Pedro's toothy, ferocious grin, he screamed and lost his grip on the ladder!

In the living room, Sam and his parents were talking to Mr. Kroop. He had neatly placed a stack of papers on the coffee table.

"And I'll need you to sign these documents," Mr. Kroop told the Cortezes. Papi had had enough. He jumped up on the table and stood on the stack of papers.

Mr. Kroop eyed Papi nervously. "Okay, buddy, get down. These are important papers."

Papi lifted up his leg, ready to pee.

"You wouldn't dare," Mr. Kroop threatened.

"Just try me, cat man," Papi growled. He lifted his leg higher. He watched the veins in Mr. Kroop's face bulge. And then he peed!

As Mr. Kroop watched, stunned, Papi snatched the bank manager's cell phone.

"My phone!" Mr. Kroop shouted. "You'll get slobber all over it!" He ran out the door after Papi. Chloe nudged a skateboard Mr. Kroop's way. He tripped over it and fell right on his back.

Furious, Mr. Kroop got up and tried unsuccessfully to clean himself off. His suit was ripped, and he had prickly thorns from the tree outside stuck to him. He was fuming as he walked back inside to the Cortez family. "This place is a *madhouse!*" he roared. "I am *officially* evicting you from this property!"

"But we still have three weeks!" Sam cried.

"Please, sir, you can't do this to us!" Mrs. Cortez protested.

"Oh, yes, I can," Mr. Kroop told them. "Your dogs are ruining this house, and this house is about to belong to the bank. I could have the sheriff here—get you all arrested for destroying bank property. I want you out by tonight." Mr. Kroop headed toward the front door. Before he exited, he turned sharply around. He reached down and grabbed the bank pen from the table. "And I'll take this back, thank you very much!" he huffed.

Before leaving, he looked at his cell phone, which he had managed to retrieve. "Who called Mexico?" he asked, frowning. Then he stormed out.

"My cousin in Tijuana says hi," Papi told the other dogs.

Mrs. Cortez looked at her husband and son. "What are we going to do? Are we supposed to sleep in the streets?" she asked, very upset.

The dogs all glanced at one another. This mission definitely had not gone as planned.

CHAPTER SIX

Later that day, the Cortez family and all the dogs were back at Aunt Vivian's mansion in Beverly Hills. The puppies were thrilled to be back home. They went yapping toward their toys, eager to play.

Mr. and Mrs. Cortez were completely in awe of how enormous the house was. "How many people live here?" Mr. Cortez asked, bewildered.

"One," Sam replied.

"Is she a giant?" his mother asked.

Sam remained quiet. He picked up his parents' bags to take to their room.

After they had all settled in, Sam and his parents sat at the large dining table with a gourmet lunch spread out before them. There was a heavy silence in the room, and no one was eating. Even the dogs sat in front of untouched bowls of food.

Sam tried to make some conversation with his parents. "This place is something, huh, Ma?" he said, attempting to lighten the mood at the table. "Even the doghouse is bigger than our place."

"Our house might be small, Sam, but it's our home. I mean, *was* . . ." Mrs. Cortez said as her eyes filled with tears. This was all too much for her. "Excuse me, please," she said, and walked out of the room.

Sam glanced over at his father. "I was just trying to cheer her up," he explained.

"I'll go talk to her," Mr. Cortez said. He got up and went after her.

Alone at the table, Sam shook his head. He picked up the newspaper in front of him and started to read.

A picture in the paper caught Chloe's attention. "Hey!" she cried.

Chloe stood in front of Sam to get a better look at the newspaper. There on the cover was Appoline, the snooty show dog from the park. She was posing for the camera with her trophy. Under the photo was the headline: BEVERLY HILLS DOG SHOW IN JUST THREE WEEKS! WILL APPOLINE WIN THE $50,000 PRIZE AGAIN?

Papi was thrilled. If they won the top prize at the dog show, they could help Sam and his family! "My love, you're a genius," Papi gushed. "If we win, the money would save the house!"

As Chloe looked at the photograph, she imagined Appoline's reaction to seeing her at the show. Chloe imagined what the show dog would say to her. "You sink you could *vin zee* dog show? Impossible! It is always *moi*. Do not make me laugh," Appoline howled. "Chihuahua? More like Chi-*ha-ha*!"

"Everything okay?" Papi asked his wife.

Just thinking of Appoline made Chloe angry. "We're going to do this! Let's tell Sam!" Chloe declared.

Chloe and Papi looked at each other and nodded. It was time to put their plan into action! They both barked loudly at Sam to get his attention.

"Whoa," Sam said, confused about the noise. "What's gotten into you two?" He put his paper down to see what Chloe and Papi were doing. Chloe was in the same pose as Appoline in the paper. She held her nose high and had one paw up in the air. Then she barked loudly again.

"I want to do the dog show!" she told Sam.

"Look at you posing," Sam said, smiling. He thought Chloe was trying to cheer him up. But then Chloe put her paw on the paper, and Sam looked down. "'Dog show,'" he read. And slowly he understood. "Wait. Oh, my gosh! Great idea, Chloe!"

Chloe grinned. "Finally," she said with a sigh of relief. Then she shook her head. "Guys are so slow."

CHAPTER SEVEN

The Beverly Hills Dog Show was in full swing. Pedigree pets and their owners were running around frantically, getting ready for the contest. Last-minute grooming checks, trick practice, and costume fixes all made for a busy preshow. The dogs were trying to psych themselves into winning.

"So this is the big league," Papi commented.

Sam was amazed by the whole scene. He leaned over to his father. "Is it me, or is it hard to tell the dogs from their owners?" he asked.

Papi looked around and noticed that many owners *did* bear a strong resemblance to their dogs. A sheepdog had the same frizzy white hair as its owner; a thin greyhound stood next to a very tall, wiry man; and a man walking with a basset hound had the same droopy expression on his face.

"Let's go sign in," Sam said to his family.

"May I help you?" a man sitting at the registration table asked Sam.

"I hope so," Sam answered cheerfully. "We're here for the dog show."

Judge McKible looked down his nose to look at the dogs. "With *these* dogs?" he asked in a snobby tone as he sized up Chloe, Papi, Delgado, and Pedro. "This is a *very* prestigious dog show. Dogs train for *years* to be prepared. I'm not sure you *or* your dogs have got what it takes."

"Well, I think we just might surprise you,"

Sam said with a pleasant smile, trying to stay positive.

The snooty judge shook his head. "I doubt it," he said. "In the meantime, you can fill out these forms." He handed Sam some papers and then quickly moved on to the next contestant. "Oh, hellooo!" he exclaimed, greeting the next owner with much more hospitality.

"Remember, Papi, they're just as nervous as you are," Papi said quietly to himself.

While Sam filled out the forms, Papi checked out the competition. A Chinese crested sighed and complained out loud, "Ugh! I'm having such a bad-hair day!" A shar-pei was examining herself in the mirror. "Is that another wrinkle? Oh, no!" she cried. Papi decided to approach a glamorous-looking shih tzu with very long hair.

"*Por favor,* senorita, do you know where we line up to go onstage?" The shih tzu barked and then turned around. Papi realized he had been talking to the back of her! "This is awkward," he said, embarrassed. "I'll just figure it out myself."

Just then, Appoline spotted Papi and recognized the dogs from the park. "*Ewww,*" she howled. "Do I smell *garbage*? No, it *iz* just *zee* peasant dogs!"

A bunch of fancy-looking dogs nearby laughed at Appoline's joke.

Papi couldn't help himself. "*We're* the ones that smell?" he asked. "You know, there's a reason poodle starts with the word *poo*."

All of the dogs couldn't help but laugh at Papi's joke. But they stopped laughing when they saw Appoline's angry expression!

Back at the mansion, Chloe and Papi's puppies, Sebastian, Biminy, and Delta were staring at the television, watching the dog show.

"When's it going to start? When? When?" Pep asked excitedly.

"Oh, they just *have* to win," Biminy said. "I've got all my paws crossed."

Delta scratched her paws on the carpet. "This is more nerve-racking than a trip to the vet," she whined.

"Everybody, shush!" Sebastian scolded.

On the screen, the host of the show, Sterling Reed, appeared with his co-host Polly Wickham. "And the twenty-fifth annual Beverly Hills Dog Show is now underway!" Sterling announced. The ballroom was dark, and spotlights swooped over the crowd. Sebastian, Delta, and Biminy cheered.

"Hundred of canines will compete in the categories of beauty, style, and talent to win the honor of top dog and a grand prize of fifty thousand dollars!" Sterling cried. He shivered. "Ooh, I've got goose bumps!" He turned to Polly. "Look! I really do!"

"You sure do, Sterling. Ooh, here comes Judge McKible. Let's hope he's in a good mood," Polly said.

Judge McKible entered the room and took a seat at the judges' table.

"Is everybody ready to win this thing and save our house?" Sam asked the dogs backstage.

The dogs all barked in agreement.

"Hands and paws in!" Sam shouted.

"*Viva el Cortez!*" the dogs cried as they piled on top of each other.

"And we're off with the first round: beauty!" Sterling announced. "Let's see those Beverly Hills dogs strut their stuff. Yowsa!"

The dogs lined up and walked down a runway as the judges nodded their heads yes or no.

Chloe and Papi turned on the charm as they walked past the judges. Even Pedro had poise as he strutted down the catwalk. Then came Delgado, followed by Appoline.

"Ugh! Zees judge had no taste! Your friends—they are trash," she whispered loud enough so Delgado could hear. Angered,

Delgado turned around and growled fiercely at Appoline.

Noticing this, Judge McKible gave Delgado a wag of his finger, and the German shepherd was eliminated! Appoline laughed haughtily while curtseying in front of the judge. He gave her a definitive nod "yes." And with that, the beauty round was over.

"The competition is getting fierce!" Sterling Reed announced. "And so are the outfits! It's time for the second round: style!"

Loud pop music filled the ballroom, and the dogs entered in wild costumes and hairstyles. Pedro was dressed as a big flower. He strutted proudly across the floor, and the audience applauded.

"You like me! You *really* like me!" Pedro cried, his eyes sparkling.

Papi knew what was about to happen. He had to stop Pedro! He shouted loudly over the music. "Wait! Don't do it, Pedro! Just don't—"

But it was too late—Pedro was already sporting his scary smile! The crowd gasped in horror at the sight. Judge McKible took one look at Pedro and shouted, "Disqualified!"

Appoline, dressed like Marie Antoinette in a fancy outfit made of lace, came out next. The judge and the crowd quickly recovered from Pedro and welcomed Appoline. Judge McKible gave an enthusiastic nod.

Chloe was up next. She knew that she had this style part nailed! Mrs. Cortez walked onstage, pulling Chloe in a wagon that was decorated like a cloud. Chloe was wearing shimmering wings and a halo. She was a truly *angelic* vision.

Papi beamed with pride and then made *his* grand entrance. Tribal music beat through the ballroom speakers, and a large screen with an image of an Aztec temple appeared. The audience went wild for Papi—he looked like a real Chihuahua warrior!

At the end of the round, there were

only five dogs left in the competition.

Polly looked to the stage. "Those hoops and batons can only mean one thing . . . we're on to the talent portion of the show!" she announced.

Some talents won over the judges, and some bored them. When a Pekingese did a handstand, Judge McKible rolled his eyes. He had seen *that* old trick before! But Sterling Reed and Polly Wickham cheered with delight when Appoline dipped her paws into paint and created a painting that looked like it belonged in a museum!

Judge McKible gave an enthusiastic thumbs-up and passed the prestigious poodle on to the next round.

"That Appoline is a regular *Pet*casso!" Sterling joked.

Polly eagerly looked over to see what Chloe would perform. Chloe sat in front of a miniature piano and played a beautiful song. The crowd cheered for her, but Judge

McKible was not impressed. With a shake of his head, he dismissed her.

Papi was outraged! He charged out into the center of the ring, barking loudly.

"How dare you!" he shouted. "Chloe is the most *beautiful*, the most *stylish*, and the most *talented* dog in the entire world!" he declared. "She has a coat like the whitest of snow, eyes that sparkle like diamonds, ears as delicate as silk, and a heart as big as, well . . . as big as . . . Why don't I just show you!"

Chloe was touched at Papi's outburst, but nervous about what he would do next. "Papi, what are you doing?" she cried. She watched Papi race over to a bouquet of roses sitting in a large vase. He skillfully ripped the rose petals off with his mouth. He darted over to Chloe with the rose petals. And one by one, he dropped the roses in a heart around his wife.

"A heart as big as this one!" Papi shouted to the audience. "*Mi amor,* Chloe, will live in my heart forever!" He bowed down in front of Chloe.

The audience leaped to their feet and cheered as Papi barked. Judge McKible looked at Papi and smiled.

"Now *that's* talent!" he shouted. He nodded his head to Papi, waving him through to the next round.

Appoline turned her head in disgust while the audience chanted, "Papi! Papi!"

"Oh, Papi, *ti adore*," Chloe said, gazing lovingly into Papi's eyes.

"Well it looks like Appoline's got some serious competition this year, and his name is Papi!" Polly observed.

"I LOVE YOU, PAPI!" Sterling Reed shouted.

Judge McKible reviewed his notes and moved closer to the microphone. "Ladies and gentlemen, I have chosen this year's finalists," he said to the audience. "They are Appoline Bouvier and Papi Cortez."

The audience exploded in a roar of applause. While Sam and everyone else was celebrating, Appoline's owner, Colleen Mansfield, pulled the judge aside and whispered something to him. Judge McKible looked through a stack of papers on his desk and then walked over to Sam.

"Mr. Cortez," the judge said right near a microphone so everyone in the room was able to hear, "you know the Beverly Hills Dog Show is for purebreds only. Do you have Papi's birth papers showing his pedigree?"

"No," Sam replied. "We rescued Papi from the pound. He was a stray."

"I *knew* it!" Colleen shouted, a huge smirk on her face.

Realizing that the microphone was on, Sam picked it up and spoke directly to the audience. "He might not have breeding papers or be a pedigree," he said, "but you'll never meet a dog that shows more heart than Papi!"

Cheers from the audience filled the arena.

Judge McKible took the microphone from Sam. "I'm sorry, but rules are rules," he said. "Papi Cortez has been disqualified due to lack of breeding papers."

The audience booed loudly.

"The winner of the twenty-fifth annual Beverly Hills Dog Show for the fourth year in a row is . . . Appoline Bouvier!" the judge announced.

As Appoline trotted to the podium to get her trophy, the audience was still booing the judge's decision.

"What? You can't do that!" Mr. and Mrs. Cortez exclaimed. They were shocked at the news!

Back at home, Sebastian, Biminy, Delta, and the puppies couldn't believe what had just happened.

"This is *loco*!" the puppies shouted. The Cortezes were going to lose their house!

In the backstage ballroom at the dog show, Sam petted Papi. "It's okay, boy. You did your best out there. We're still a family and that's all that matters," he said sincerely.

Chloe trotted up to Papi. "You're the love of my life, Papi. I have never been prouder of you than I am today," she told him.

Sam scooped up Papi. Then he, his parents, and Chloe headed for the exit. As they made their way past the other dogs and owners, Papi saw Appoline, who was with her owner and her shiny trophy. Appoline noticed Papi, too. She bowed her head in respect. Papi jumped out of Sam's arms and scurried through the crowd to get to her.

"Appoline," he said, coming up to her, "I know we haven't always seen snout to snout, but you were great out there." Papi started to walk away, but Appoline suddenly stopped him.

"Papi! I may have won *zee* trophy, but I'd give all *zat* up to have a family like yours.

You're a lucky dog," she told him. "For a peasant," she added.

"I guess I am," Papi replied, smiling. "See you at the dog park. This time, say hi."

Sam came over to Papi. "You ready, champ?"

"Champ? *Please!*" Appoline's owner spat. "He lost. The money is ours!"

"Yeah, and look how unhappy you still are. We may not have the prize, but we have each other," Sam told her. Then he went to rejoin his family, who beamed at him proudly.

Mr. Cortez put his arm around Sam. "Well said, my son," he told Sam.

And with that, the Cortez family walked out.

CHAPTER EIGHT

When everyone returned to Aunt Viv's house, Papi snuck into the puppies' room to watch his children sleep. Before he turned to leave, Papi Jr. called to him.

"Sorry to wake you, son. Go back to bed," Papi whispered.

"We can't sleep," Ali reported, popping her head up.

"Yeah, we're too upset. We don't want your family to lose their house," Papi Jr. told him.

"I know, my *niños*," Papi replied sympathetically. "That's because you are very loyal to those you love dearly. Just like the Chihuahua warriors!"

"Tell us another story, Daddy!" Pep pleaded.

Papi sighed. His stories had gotten them all into too much trouble already. "If you promise to go right back to bed, I'll tell you a story," Papi said.

The puppies sat up eagerly.

"You see, the Chihuahua warriors, they were not just brave and passionate. They were also fiercely loyal," Papi told his children.

"They were?" Lala asked.

"Oh, yes," Papi said. "And our ancestors were not only loyal to their fellow Chihuahuas, they were to their humans. In ancient times, they used to follow their humans into battle."

Papi went on to describe a raging battle

in which the king's brave Chihuahua raced through the fields to find his master. "They knew that even in times of great danger they must stand by their friends and warn them of their attacking enemies. Even at the risk of their own lives." Papi took a moment to look at his pups.

"That Chihuahua saved the king's life?" Papi Jr. asked.

Papi nodded. "Yes," he said. "Stick by your loved ones, even in hard times. We are stronger together than we are alone."

"From now on, we'll be the most loyal Chihuahuas ever," Papi Jr. vowed. "And we'll never give up."

"I know you won't," Papi said softly. "Sleep tight."

As the puppies said good night and closed their eyes, Papi stood at the door watching them all drift off to sleep. He walked down the hallway, and paused when he spotted Mr. Cortez comforting his wife on the couch.

Mrs. Cortez was very upset. Pedro laid his head in her lap, and she hugged him tightly. Papi continued down the hall. Sam was in his room. Sam took a deep breath and then dialed his phone.

In the rain forest, Rachel had just pushed through the branches of a large Kapok tree to photograph a plant. She smiled as she snapped a picture. At that moment, a man brought her a cell phone. She handed her camera to him and eagerly took the phone. She was hoping it was Sam.

And it was! "Sam! How'd it go?" she asked anxiously.

"Not so good," Sam replied regretfully. He paced around his bedroom at the mansion.

"Oh, no," Rachel replied.

"And now we have two days to pack up the house and move on," he explained.

"Oh, Sam," Rachel said sadly.

"I'm going to Arizona for a little while to

get them set up," he continued. "I already contacted Viv's housekeeper about watching the dogs."

"I can come, too, if you want," Rachel offered.

"No, that's okay," he said. "This is a family thing."

Rachel was stunned by Sam's words. "I thought we *were* family," she said quietly. "You know, that we would get married and have kids . . ." her voice trailed off.

Sam kept walking nervously around the room. "Rach," he said softly, "I—I love you, but I don't know if I can marry you. I can't take care of you and a family when I can hardly take care of the one I already have."

Trying to fight back tears, Rachel was grateful this was a phone conversation so Sam wouldn't see her cry. "Oh. I see . . . Um," she stammered. "I should go. Work, you know . . . Good-bye, Sam."

"Good-bye, Rachel," Sam told her.

Rachel hung up quickly. She leaned against a tree for support. Sam's words had stung. She wished that she could have talked to him in person.

Papi watched Sam stare at the phone in his hand. He walked over to him. "Love—so easy to feel, so hard to get right," he said sympathetically.

Then he went to look for Chloe. He found her sitting at the window, gazing down at the gardens. Papi came up behind her and noticed that she was watching Delgado pace back and forth.

"Looks like he could use a friend," Papi observed.

Chloe knew Papi was right. The two dogs went outside together to talk to Delgado.

"You okay, *amigo*?" Papi asked as they approached.

"Yeah, sure," the proud German shepherd said.

Chloe stepped forward. "Oh, Delgado, I

wish you would open up to me. Won't you tell us what happened with your sons?" she asked.

"We're your friends. You can trust us," Papi said, urging him to confide in them.

Delgado sighed. He took a deep breath and began to tell them the story. "About three years ago, when I was on the force in Mexico, we apprehended some really bad guys," he said. "We also got their dogs. Those dogs threatened my family. Said they'd get back at me by hurting my pups. So I took my boys out of the country and to Los Angeles."

The memory of walking away from his pups was still vivid in Delgado's mind. He had hidden in the bushes next to the police station and waited until a police officer took the basket of puppies inside. "I thought they'd be safer away from me," he whispered. "It was the hardest thing I've ever done." He looked down sadly as he remembered the sound of his young pups whimpering. He had run away fast and forced himself not to turn and look at them. "Don't turn around, don't turn around," he had told himself. Delgado looked off into the distance. "As you remember, the police force let me go when my partner got injured. I went into hiding, and I lost contact with my sons. When I was finally reinstated, I knew I had to find them again. But now they want nothing to do with me. They think I abandoned them for no reason."

"But if you tell them what happened, they'll understand," Papi assured Delgado.

"I think it's time to just let go. Seems like we're all losing what's dear to us," Delgado replied sadly.

As Delgado slumped away, Chloe and Papi shared a concerned look. The two Chihuahuas didn't realize it, but Papi Jr. had been listening to the whole conversation from the doorway.

"Poor Delgado," the puppy said quietly to

himself. "We've got to do something to help him." He raced back upstairs to his sisters before his parents saw him.

The next morning, just as the sun was coming up, Papi heard Chloe shout from the puppies' room.

"Papi! Come quick!" she cried frantically. "The puppies are gone!"

Papi rushed into the puppies' bedroom with Pedro and Delgado close behind.

"Maybe they're hiding somewhere," Pedro suggested.

The dogs barked as they searched the room. Delgado stopped and held his nose high in the air.

"No," he said. "They left the house."

"But where could they have gone?" Chloe asked, very frightened and worried.

Chloe would never have guessed where her children were headed. Papi Jr. led his sisters to the back fence of the Beverly Hills police station. The five puppies stood at the fence watching the police dogs training.

"Okay, this is where Uncle Delgado said his sons worked. We'll just tell them the truth, and then they'll forgive him," Papi Jr. said.

"This is scary," Lala said. "We've never been out by ourselves before."

"Don't you want to be *real* Chihuahua warriors, like the ones in Dad's stories, instead of just make-believe?" Papi Jr. asked, looking at his sisters.

"Yeah!" the girls cheered.

The puppies squeezed under the fence to get closer to Delgado's sons. Suddenly, a call for help came over a walkie-talkie. "Attention all units, attention all units. We have a robbery in progress at Southcoast Bank. All units respond."

"We've got a situation, everybody!" the officer shouted to the group. "Round up the dogs and let's move out!"

The police officers grabbed their gear and rushed to their vehicles. Delgado's sons ran toward the parking lot along with the officers.

"Hey, those dogs have the same scent as Uncle Delgado!" Papi Jr. exclaimed, spotting two young German shepherds. "That must be them!"

Papi Jr. and his sisters raced after the dogs and into a police van. As soon as they stepped inside, Alberto, one of Delgado's sons, looked up. "Hey, what are you doing in here? This is police property," he said sternly.

"We're friends with your dad, and we've got something to tell you," Papi Jr. said.

Before the dogs could say another word, the van sped off to the crime scene. Minutes later, the door opened and the officer ordered the police dogs to track the scent of the criminals.

Alberto and Antonio leaped out of the van,

ready to get to work. Alberto looked back over his shoulder. "We'll talk more about this after," he told the puppies. "Stay here. We don't want you getting hurt."

"Oh, no!" Pep cried as the dogs ran off. "We didn't tell them Uncle Delgado is leaving LA soon. Come on!"

"Then let's tell them now," Papi Jr. said. He took off after the brothers with his four sisters following him.

Back at the mansion, Mrs. Cortez sat on the couch with Chloe. She was organizing flyers to hand out about the lost puppies while Sam spoke on the phone.

He paused and then frowned. "Well, if you see them, give us a call," he said.

"Any news?" Mr. Cortez asked as Sam hung up the phone.

Sam shook his head.

Mr. Cortez moved closer to the television. The news was on, and he squinted at the screen to get a better look. "Hey! Isn't that our bank?" he asked. He leaned over to turn up the volume.

There on the news was the Southcoast bank! Policemen surrounded the building, and a newscaster stood in front reporting from the scene.

"And according to police, the robbers are still inside," the newsman said. "At this time, there are no hostages."

As the man reported the news on-screen, the five puppies snuck behind him. Sam pointed to the television.

"Did I just see what I think I saw?" Sam asked in amazement.

Chloe sat up and barked. "Yes! It's them!"

"I'm off to the bank!" Sam shouted, grabbing his car keys. "Mom, Dad, you stay here in case anyone gets to them first and calls."

"Of course," his father responded.

As Sam opened the front door, Chloe, Papi,

Pedro, and Delgado rushed out ahead of him.

"I guess this is a family affair," Sam said. Everyone piled into Sam's car and they took off.

There was a large crowd around the front doors of the bank. The five puppies scanned the crowd.

"I don't see Delgado's sons," Papi Jr. said worriedly. "Where'd they go?"

Ali nodded toward the bank. "I bet they went that way," she suggested.

"Nah, I bet they went *that* way," Rosa said, spotting an alley across the street. "I'm always right. Follow me!"

"Oh, no! What if we never find them?" Lala asked. She looked at her siblings and saw their worried faces. "I mean, of *course* we'll find them," she said, trying to remain positive. "We're warriors!"

"Antonio? Alberto?" Papi Jr. called. "Are you here?"

Suddenly, a manhole cover on the ground popped open. A heavy bag flew out, landing right in front of the puppies.

"Presents!" Pep cried out. "Oh, boy! Is it Christmas?"

Papi Jr. cautiously approached the bag. He sniffed it and then stuck his head inside. When his head appeared again, his mouth held a wad of green bills! "Hey, look!" he cried. "This is what everyone's been saying we need. We can save the house with this!"

Before his sisters could respond, two more bags were tossed out of the manhole.

"Everyone get as much of it as you can," Papi Jr. instructed.

The puppies all dove inside the bags to get the cash. Just at that moment, one of the robbers popped out of the manhole.

He took off his mask and looked over at the bank, which was surrounded by police. "Good work in there, boys," he said to his cohorts. "Let's move out!"

The three crooks grabbed the bags full of money—with the puppies inside—and threw them into a truck that was waiting in the alley.

In a flash, the truck sped off with the bank's money—and the five puppies!

"What's happening? Where are we going? Who turned out the lights?" the puppies asked each other.

As the van sped off, a police officer shouted into his walkie-talkie. "Gone?" he cried. "Are you sure? But that's impossible!" He turned to the other cops. "The robbers got away somehow. Let's move in!" he ordered.

CHAPTER NINE

Sam's car pulled up to the curb in front of the Southcoast Bank. He jumped out of the car. "You guys wait here," he said to the dogs. He closed the door and headed over to the crowd of police.

"No way!" Papi cried. "Those are my kids in there! Come on, let's go!" He leaped out of the car window with Chloe, Delgado, and Pedro right behind him.

As Sam walked up to the crowd, the television reporter was interviewing Mr. Kroop.

"There were at least fifteen to twenty of them," Mr. Kroop said, still frazzled from his ordeal inside the bank. "They were fast."

Sam walked past Mr. Kroop, making his way to the bank. A police officer noticed him and went running over.

"Sir, I have to ask you to step back," the officer said. "This is a crime scene."

"Right. Sorry," Sam told him. "It's just . . . did you happen to see five Chihuahua puppies around here?"

"Puppies?" The officer asked in a tone that suggested he clearly thought Sam was crazy.

Meanwhile, Chloe, Papi, Delgado, and Pedro were not wasting any time. With Delgado's keen sense of smell, he led the others across the street into the alley. "I got their scent. Come on!" he called. Delgado sniffed the air as he walked around the alley. "They were just here."

Pedro found the mask that one of the

robbers had thrown off when he escaped from the manhole. He carried it over to Delgado.

"It smells like . . ." Delgado began, sniffing.

"Pepperoni!" Papi shouted.

"But what does that mean? Where are the kids?" Chloe asked.

"I know who can help us," Delgado said seriously. He led his friends inside the bank where he knew they'd find Alberto and Antonio. The two dogs were hard at work, sniffing for clues.

Chloe noticed that Delgado looked a little nervous about approaching his sons. She walked up to her dear friend. "I'll be right behind you," she told him.

Delgado walked toward the dogs, with Chloe right near him. Antonio looked up, surprised to see Delgado. He had immediately recognized him as his father.

"Dad, what are you—" Antonio began to ask.

"I know you don't want to see me right now," Delgado cut in. "But I've got some missing puppies and I'm following a lead."

"We told them to wait in the van!" Antonio cried.

"Well, they didn't, and we have to find them. We found this mask—smells like pepperoni. Any ideas?" He placed the ski mask in front of his son.

Alberto came over and smelled the clue. "Pepperoni . . ." he said, thinking.

"Of course!" Antonio cried as he remembered something. "There's a pizza factory not far from here."

"How do we get there?" Delgado asked.

"It's pretty close. Just head north until you smell soap, then make a left at sweaty socks and cross the street. You get a big waft of pepperoni on that corner. If you smell doughnuts, you've gone too far," Antonio replied.

Delgado shook his head. "I have no idea what you just said."

"He said go north until you hit the Laundromat. Make a left at the gym and then cross the street. If we hit the bakery, we've gone past it," Chloe translated.

"Wow! Impressive, kid," Delgado told her.

Antonio sprung into action. "We'll grab the humans and meet you there!" he announced.

Delgado and his sons looked at each other for a moment with understanding. And then the police dogs ran off to find the officers.

"Follow me," Delgado said to Papi, Pedro, and Chloe. And with that, the four dogs raced out of the bank toward the pizza factory.

Sam saw his dogs run off. "Where are they going?" he asked out loud. Then he raced to follow them.

The robbers pulled up in front of a large brick building. The men jumped out of the truck and quickly carried the bags inside. One man dumped his bag on a table—and wads of money fell out. The men were so intent on counting the cash in that bag, they didn't even notice that the other two bags were squirming on the floor.

"Better get back into uniform before the foreman sees we've been gone," one of the crooks said.

The other two slipped on their jumpsuits so it would look as if they had been at work the whole time.

"Like he'd ever notice. How many of these jobs have we pulled off the last few months?" one of them said, cackling.

"Yeah!" his partner said, laughing. "We just press the ON button, and the machines do all the work. It's the perfect cover for our little extracurricular activities."

Proud of themselves for another bank heist, the men laughed as they counted their cash.

At the front entrance of the factory,

Delgado sniffed the air. "This smells like the place," he announced to his friends.

"Pepperoni!" Papi, Chloe, and Pedro shouted.

"Let's go get your kids!" Delgado ordered and headed into the factory.

Pedro paused. "Those guys in there could be dangerous. Do you have some kind of plan?"

"Don't I always, *hermano*?" Papi replied confidently.

Inside, the robbers continued to divide up the cash from the first bag. Then one of them unzipped the second bag. Suddenly, Papi Jr. jumped out!

"Huh?" the man yelped, surprised to see a puppy leap out of the bag.

Papi Jr. stood bravely, barking at the men. "Back off, mister! You can't kidnap us and get away with it! Don't mess with us! We're Chihuahua warriors."

The three men stared at the yapping puppy. Then they realized there was more barking coming from the other bags. They opened the sacks and four puppy heads peeked out.

Papi Jr. growled, trying to look fierce. The three crooks jumped back.

"Wow! I'm really good!" Papi Jr. boasted. What he didn't realize was that Pedro was right behind him, showing off his ferocious grin. The men were staring at Pedro standing in the doorway.

"Back away from the puppies," Pedro growled. "And in case you were wondering," he added, "this *isn't* a smile!"

Papi Jr. spun around. "Uncle Pedro?" he shouted. "You found us!" He stopped for a minute and added, "I mean, not that we needed help or anything."

Pedro growled at the crooks again. Papi Jr. ran over to him and tried to make his tiny growl just as mean.

"Calm down now. Nice doggy," one of the crooks said.

"Who are you calling nice?" Pedro said, and charged into the room.

The crooks quickly scooped up the three bags of money with Papi Jr.'s sisters still inside.

"Help!" the girl puppies cried.

"Now for phase two," Pedro said confidently to Papi Jr.

"But they're getting away!" Papi Jr. protested.

"They won't get far," Pedro promised.

He knew that Delgado and Chloe were hiding out behind some boxes. With their teeth, they each held on to one end of a long string of pepperoni.

"Here they come! Ready?" Delgado said as he saw one of the robbers rush toward them.

"Ready!" Chloe replied.

"Pull!" Delgado commanded.

The two friends each yanked on one end of the string. As the robber came running toward them, he didn't have time to stop and he tripped right over the line. He hurtled forward and crashed into a huge vat of tomato sauce!

"Never mess with a Chihuahua!" Chloe cried.

"Hey!" Delgado said defensively.

"Right," Chloe said, nodding. "Or a German shepherd!" she added.

The bag of money that the man was carrying fell near them. Rosa's and Lala's heads popped out.

"Thank goodness you're okay!" Chloe cried when she saw her pups.

"Mom! Delgado!" Rosa and Lala called as they came rushing forward.

Chloe showered her girls with kisses. She looked up at Delgado. "Looks like our partnership still works," she said with a little grin.

"Yeah," Delgado agreed. "But let's not

make a habit of this rescuing thing. It's exhausting."

While Chloe and Delgado were talking, the other two crooks were racing toward the factory exit. Just as they reached the door, they were pelted with tomatoes! As they turned to see where the tomatoes had come from, they spotted Papi high in a tomato crate, digging with his paws at superspeed.

"No one messes with my kids!" Papi yelled heroically.

The two men staggered backward and dropped the bags. Ali and Rosa peered out.

Suddenly, Papi dove off the crate and flew through the air in a high arched jump. His paw reached out and hit a button on the wall before he gracefully landed. A vat of gooey pizza dough was dumped on the two men. "I have a feeling this isn't exactly what these guys had in mind when they thought they'd be 'rolling in the dough,'" Papi said, laughing at his own joke.

"Wow, Dad!" Rosa exclaimed.

"That was amazing!" Ali cheered.

Papi looked at his daughters. "I'm just glad you're okay," he said, relieved.

Just then, the police officers appeared with Alberto and Antonio in the lead. The policemen handcuffed the dough-covered crooks as the dogs looked on happily.

"Great work!" Alberto told the group.

"That was awesome!" Papi Jr. exclaimed. "We were just like the Chihuahua warriors, weren't we, Mom?"

"You did a very dangerous thing today, kids. I'd be upset with you if I wasn't so proud. You're my brave little Chihuahuas," Chloe told her puppies.

"The bravest!" Papi added.

"They take after you, Papi," Chloe said, looking at her husband. "You're the most loving, loyal, and brave Chihuahua I know, and you've taught our children to be the same way."

"But I still have a problem keeping them in line," Papi replied, shaking his head.

"I think together we make a pretty good team," Chloe said with a smile. "We kicked some butt in there today!"

"Right!" Papi exclaimed, perking up. "Who needs a Chihuahua warrior when you have a Chihuahua *family*!"

The whole family nuzzled together happily.

"Got room for one more in there?" Pedro asked, then jumped in and joined the pile.

Outside, Chloe saw Delgado standing far away from the pizza-factory exit. She knew that he was waiting for his sons and that he was nervous. Then she saw Antonio and Alberto coming out of the factory.

Delgado spotted them and started to walk away. "Don't turn around, don't turn around," he said to himself.

"Dad! Wait!" Alberto called, rushing toward his father.

"I think we owe you an apology," Antonio added.

"The puppies told us why you left," Alberto said.

"We didn't know it was to protect us. Thank you, Dad," Antonio said.

"I hope it's not too late to be a family again," Delgado told his sons hopefully.

"Nothing would make us happier," Alberto answered with a smile.

Chloe sighed as she watched her friend and his sons.

A police officer approached Delgado. "You're quite the police dog, fella. Let's see who you belong to." He reached down to check Delgado's tags. "Mexican police force?" he said. "I wonder if they'd let us borrow you for a little while. We could sure use your nose on a couple of cases." He petted Delgado on the head. "What do you think of that, boys?"

Alberto and Antonio started to bark their approval enthusiastically.

"Let me give them a call," the police officer said.

Delgado looked at his sons. "You want me to stay?"

"Yeah, I think we have a lot of catching up to do," Alberto replied.

"It's great to have you back, Dad," Antonio chimed in.

Chloe stepped forward. "It looks like you're going to be a Beverly Hills dog, Delgado!"

"Thank you for everything, *princessa*," Delgado said, full of gratitude. "You have a beautiful family. And thanks to them, I have my family back, too."

"I'm sure I'll see you around, Delgado," Chloe told her friend. "How about we meet up next year to do the dog show?"

Delgado shook his head. "In your dreams, kid!" he cried. He turned and followed his sons.

Chloe laughed and watched Delgado climb into the van. Papi, Pedro, and the puppies circled around her. And then they saw Sam! They all raced toward him excitedly.

"Foiling a bank robbery! You guys are some kind of heroes, huh?" Sam said, overjoyed to have all the dogs back together.

CHAPTER TEN

A moving van sat in front of the Cortez house, along with Sam's gardening truck, which was filled to the brim with household goods, clothing, and furniture. It was moving day, and boxes and suitcases surrounded Sam and his parents. Even the dogs were helping with the huge task of packing up. Pedro nudged a box with his head, and Chloe placed a rubber bone into an open suitcase.

Sadly, Papi watched Mrs. Cortez take a family photo off the mantel. The picture had been taken in front of the house. Pedro and Papi were in the photo as well. Mrs. Cortez placed the picture in a box.

"I've got the garage all packed up. I'll go finish the kitchen," Mr. Cortez said.

"The cousins will be here soon to pick up Pedro," Sam said to his father. "You should probably say good-bye."

Mr. Cortez kneeled down next to Pedro, tears in his eyes. "I'm going to miss you, buddy. You'll make tons of new friends in Texas—just wait a while to smile at them," he advised.

The puppies approached their father.

"I don't want Uncle Pedro to go, Papa!" Papi Jr. said sadly.

"He's not really going anywhere, kids, because when you love someone, they are always with you in your heart," Papi told his children.

"I feel the same way, *hermano*," Pedro said to Papi.

Sam sealed up the box he had been packing and silently went out to the truck. As he walked outside, he ran right into Mr. Kroop and a police officer.

"Don't worry," Sam told them. "We're leaving." He looked over at the officer. "And you didn't need to bring the police with you. We won't make any trouble."

"Please, can we come in?" Mr. Kroop asked. Sam nodded, and the men walked into the house. As they entered, the dogs growled, and Mr. Kroop stepped behind the police officer.

"You know, your dogs are pretty special," the officer said. "They solved a case that stumped a whole task force. We've been tracking those criminals for three months. They've gotten over fifteen million dollars from banks in the area."

"And there's a reward for fifty thousand dollars for their capture," Mr. Kroop added. "It's yours." He grinned sheepishly. "That's enough to pay off the loan on your house, and then some."

Papi started barking. He called the other dogs over to come hear the news.

"Is this a joke?" Mr. Cortez asked. "Because I am not laughing."

Mr. Kroop shook his head. "I promise you, Mr. Cortez, this is not a joke."

The family stood still, stunned by the turn of events.

"Holy guacamole, we did it!" Papi barked, breaking the silence. "We saved the house!"

The Cortez family laughed with joy and hugged each other while all the dogs barked excitedly. Mrs. Cortez was so elated she even hugged the officer and Mr. Kroop.

Then the dogs jumped up on Mr. Kroop, knocking him to the floor. They covered him with kisses.

"Oh, gosh! No licking!" Mr. Kroop pleaded, wiping his face. "Do they have their shots? This is my best suit!" he protested.

"What are we waiting for?" Mrs. Cortez cried. "Let's unpack!" She ran to the mantel and proudly put the family photo back up. Sam pulled out a picture of Rachel and himself and looked at it sadly.

"You need to work things out with Rachel," Mrs. Cortez advised, seeing her son's distraught face.

"I don't think so, Mom. I really messed up," Sam said. Just then, there was a knock at the door.

"Right on time," Mrs. Cortez said with a small smile. She went to get the door, and when she opened it, Rachel was standing there!

Sam's mouth dropped open in shock.

Mrs. Cortez looked at her son. "I called her. A mother wants to see her son happy."

Sam turned to Rachel "I'm so sorry, Rachel," he told her.

"No, *I'm* sorry," she said. "I hated the way we left things. I want to be with you whether we're married or not."

Sam looked at the dogs and his family. He realized that they were all staring at him. He took Rachel in his arms. "That's good. Because I want to be with you forever," he said. "I want to have a family with you and depend on each other for the rest of our lives, Rachel." Kneeling down on one knee, Sam looked up at Rachel. "Rachel, will you marry me?"

Rachel looked at the dogs. They were all wagging their tails at her.

"Yes! Yes! Of course!" she cried.

Sam picked her up and hugged her tightly while everyone cheered—and barked!

"And *I'm* throwing the wedding!" Aunt Viv exclaimed, popping her head in the door. She grinned at the happy couple.

"Viv!" Sam exclaimed, surprised but delighted to see his boss's smiling face.

"There's my Chloe!" Aunt Viv said, spotting her Chihuahua. Chloe ran up to Viv, who swept the dog up in her arms. "I've missed you so much, my darling. And there are my babies. . . . I'm so happy to meet you!" she exclaimed, petting the puppies. "Let's celebrate!" Viv cried.

Once again, Viv's backyard was the perfect location for a celebration. Music filled the air, and the guests were all enjoying a feast of fajitas and quesadillas. Everyone was dancing and having a great time. On the dance floor, Mr. and Mrs. Cortez spun in circles next to Sam and Rachel. Aunt Viv danced around holding Papi Jr. He licked her face, enjoying the love and attention.

In the pool, Pedro had his eyes closed on a raft, playing Barco Polo with the puppies.

Papi and Chloe watched the action from the back porch and smiled.

"Shall we join in the fun?" Chloe asked Papi. She moved toward the yard.

"My sweet, be careful! The mud!" Papi

warned as he spied a little puddle of mud in front of her.

Papi ran inside the house and quickly dashed back with a towel in his mouth. He placed the towel down on the puddle so Chloe could walk over it.

"Oh, Papi, you're so romantic," Chloe said, swooning.

"But of course. After all, I'm a Chihuahua," Papi replied.

"Don't I know it," Chloe said, smiling.

And together they raced off to join their happy family. It was time to celebrate!